The Berenstain Bears'
TROUBLE AT SCHOOL

VERY POOR!

When a problem at school
Is kept secret too long,
It can grow 'til a cub
Thinks that everything's <u>wrong</u>!

A FIRST TIME BOOK®

The Berenstain Bears'
TROUBLE AT SCHOOL

Stan & Jan Berenstain

Random House New York

Library of Congress Cataloging-in-Publication Data: Berenstain, Stan. The Berenstain bears' trouble at school. (A First time book) SUMMARY: When Brother Bear returns to school after being out sick, he gets into a mess that gets worse and worse until Gramps gives him some advice. [1. Bears—Fiction. 2. Schools—Fiction] I. Berenstain, Jan. II. Title. III. Series: Berenstain, Stan. First time books.   PZ7.B4483Bfl   1986   [E]   86-4999
ISBN: 0-394-87336-X (trade); 0-394-97336-4 (lib. bdg.)

Manufactured in the United States of America   24   25   26   27   28   29   30

Though Brother and Sister Bear were usually very healthy, they occasionally caught cold. So when Brother came home from school one day sneezing and wheezing, Mama Bear knew just what to do.

She took his temperature,

tucked him into bed,

and went right to the phone
and called Dr. Grizzly.

"Sneezing and wheezing and a temperature of a hundred and one?" said Dr. Grizzly. "Keep him in bed, give him plenty of liquids, and keep him home from school until his temperature is back to normal."

Mama followed the doctor's orders, and little by little Brother's temperature began to go down.

"I feel a little better," he said. "May I get out of bed?"

"I'm afraid not," said Mama. "The doctor wants you to stay in bed.

"But there's no reason why your stay shouldn't be as pleasant as possible.... Papa!" she called. "Would you bring up the portable TV?"

The portable had remote control, and pretty soon Brother was having a fine time switching from one cartoon show to another.

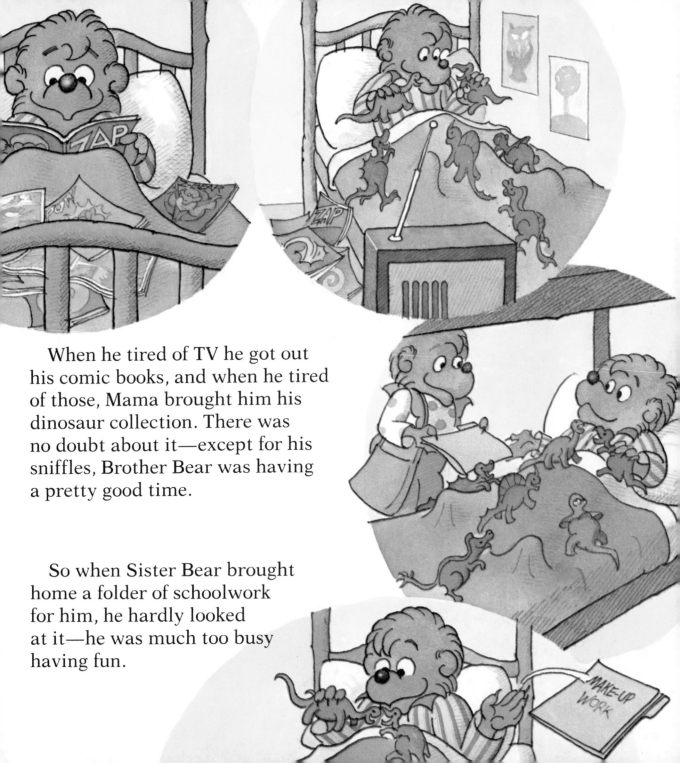

When he tired of TV he got out his comic books, and when he tired of those, Mama brought him his dinosaur collection. There was no doubt about it—except for his sniffles, Brother Bear was having a pretty good time.

So when Sister Bear brought home a folder of schoolwork for him, he hardly looked at it—he was much too busy having fun.

But while he was at home having fun, his fellow students at school were hard at work…

In the classroom, where Teacher Bob was teaching a new math lesson. They had learned to add, subtract, and multiply. Now they were learning to divide.

$$96 \div 3 =$$

$$3\overline{)96} \; 32$$

On the soccer field, where Coach Bruin was getting the team ready for the big game against Beartown…

"Cousin Freddy!" he called. "Take Brother's place at forward. He's out sick."

"Yes, sir!" said Freddy. This was the chance he'd been waiting for.

It wasn't until Brother was all better and ready to go back to school that he remembered the folder of work. "Oh well," he thought, "I'll study it on the bus."

But that's where he heard about Freddy and the soccer team. He was so upset he forgot all about studying.

When Coach Bruin had extra practice during early gym, Brother became even more upset. It wasn't easy watching Freddy take his place on the team.

Then, when Brother got back to class, Teacher Bob said, "I certainly hope you studied that work folder, because we're going to have a quiz."

"A quiz?" said Brother. "On what?"

"On division, of course," said Teacher Bob as he handed out the quiz papers.

Brother might have managed even then. He was good with numbers and might have worked things out if only he'd been able to concentrate. But all he could think about was Cousin Freddy out there kicking field goals while he sat on the bench.

The quiz was a disaster. Not only did Brother get every problem wrong, but Teacher Bob wrote on the paper: *"Very poor! Must be signed by parent."*

Brother didn't know which was worse: the soccer mess or the quiz disaster. What would he say to Mama and Papa when they asked him how things had gone at school? He was so busy feeling sorry for himself on the bus ride home that he didn't notice that Sister was coming down with a bad case of the sneezes and wheezes.

"Oh, dear!" said Mama when she saw Sister. "You've caught Brother's cold. Into bed with you!" She and Papa were so busy attending to Sister that they forgot to ask Brother how things went at school...*and he didn't tell them!*

And the next morning, when the
school bus came, *Brother didn't get on
the bus!* He hid in the tall grass until the
bus was out of sight. The squirrels
and bluebirds were puzzled—Brother
was usually happy and cheerful. But
not this morning. This morning he
looked *unhappy*—and angry, too.

"Phooey!" Brother shouted, kicking a stone. But kicking the stone reminded him of soccer and that just made him angrier. The bluebirds took off and the squirrels scattered.

"Phooey on soccer!" he shouted, stomping off through the woods. Stomp! Stomp! Stomp! Grasshoppers hopped. Toads stood stock-still and pretended they were bumps on a log.

"Phooey on school!" Brother shouted, stomping out of the woods. Pansies hid their faces. Ladybugs flew away home.

"And," he said, reaching into his schoolbag, "phooey on division!"

He had come to the top of a big hill. He
took out the quiz, folded it into a paper
airplane, and sailed it high into the air.
The hill overlooked a swampy, overgrown
bog. As Brother watched the quiz circle and
swoop he noticed something out of the
corner of his eye—a familiar house at
the edge of the bog.

Grizzly Gramps was working on a ship model when he heard the knock. Gran was making cookies. They weren't expecting visitors and they certainly weren't expecting Brother—especially during school hours.

It didn't take long for the whole story to come out. Gramps and Gran listened quietly as Brother told them about catching cold, the folder of work, the soccer mess, the quiz disaster, the missed bus, and the paper airplane.

"Come with me, young feller," said Gramps. "I want to show you something."

Gramps took Brother by the hand and led him deep into the bog.

"There!" he said. "That's what I want to show you."

It was a very old wagon sunk almost out of sight in a muddy pond.

"How did it get there?" asked Brother.

"It wasn't easy," said Gramps. "I went to a lot of trouble getting that old wagon into this swamp." Then, with a twinkle in his eye, he said, "Just the way you did getting in over your head at school!

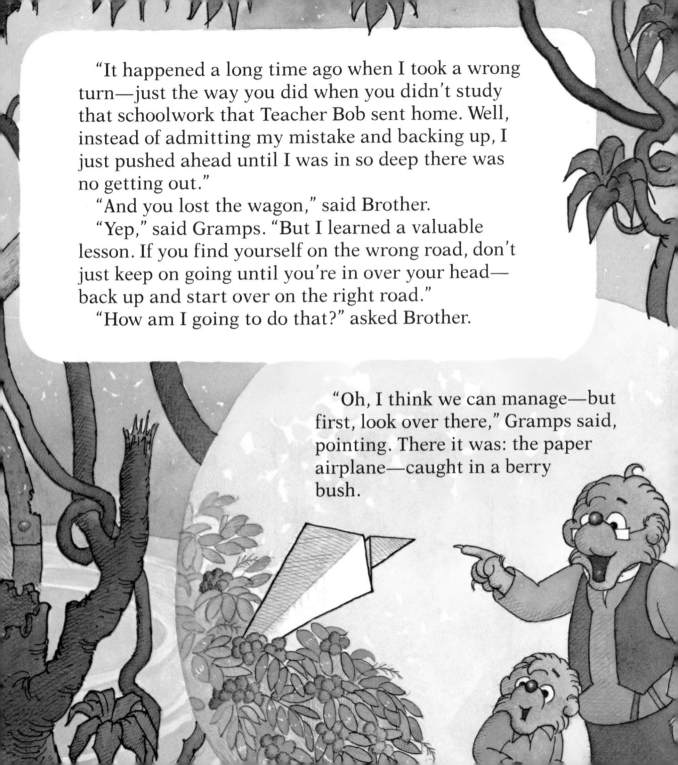

"It happened a long time ago when I took a wrong turn—just the way you did when you didn't study that schoolwork that Teacher Bob sent home. Well, instead of admitting my mistake and backing up, I just pushed ahead until I was in so deep there was no getting out."

"And you lost the wagon," said Brother.

"Yep," said Gramps. "But I learned a valuable lesson. If you find yourself on the wrong road, don't just keep on going until you're in over your head—back up and start over on the right road."

"How am I going to do that?" asked Brother.

"Oh, I think we can manage—but first, look over there," Gramps said, pointing. There it was: the paper airplane—caught in a berry bush.

"What do you think they'll say?"
asked Brother later as they
bounced along in Gramps's pickup.
"We'll find out soon enough,"
said Gramps, pulling to a stop
in front of the big tree house.
"And let's not forget Gran's bag of
cookies. They're her finest."

Mama and Papa weren't exactly pleased when they heard about the big mess Brother had gotten himself into. But they didn't holler and pound the table, either—not even Papa. He looked like he might be going to when he saw the paper he had to sign—Gramps had tried to flatten it out but it was still pretty wrinkled.

"What happened to this?" he asked.

"Oh," said Gramps. "It just sort of got folded a bit." That's when he brought out Gran's cookies. There were ten of them. "Let's see, now," he said, "there are five of us counting Sister. So how many cookies do we each get?"

"Two, of course," said Brother, dividing them up.

"Don't look now, young feller," said Gramps with a wink, "but you just divided ten by five!"

"Is that all there is to dividing?" said Brother.

"That's all," said Gramps.

"Come along," said Mama in a no-nonsense voice.

"Where are we going?"
asked Brother.

"To school," Mama said
as they got in the car.

"But it's so late,"
protested Brother.

"It's never too late to
correct a mistake," Mama
said, and off they went.

Brother got to class just in time for a retest. The class hadn't done very well on the division quiz, so Teacher Bob was giving them a second chance.

Brother really concentrated and did much better.

And that afternoon he got a second chance at soccer, too. It was the day of the big game against Beartown and things weren't going very well.

"Brother," said Coach Bruin, "I want you to go in for Freddy. I don't think he's quite ready for first team."

"Glad to help, Coach," Brother said as he ran out onto the field. "You know what they say—it's never too late to correct a mistake."